Dear Parent:
Your child's love of reading starts here!

Every child learns to read in a different way and at his or her own speed. Some go back and forth between reading levels and read favorite books again and again. Others read through each level in order. You can help your young reader improve and become more confident by encouraging his or her own interests and abilities. From books your child reads with you to the first books he or she reads alone, there are I Can Read Books for every stage of reading:

SHARED READING
Basic language, word repetition, and whimsical illustrations, ideal for sharing with your emergent reader

BEGINNING READING
Short sentences, familiar words, and simple concepts for children eager to read on their own

READING WITH HELP
Engaging stories, longer sentences, and language play for developing readers

READING ALONE
Complex plots, challenging vocabulary, and high-interest topics for the independent reader

I Can Read Books have introduced children to the joy of reading since 1957. Featuring award-winning authors and illustrators and a fabulous cast of beloved characters, I Can Read Books set the standard for beginning readers.

A lifetime of discovery begins with the magical words **"I Can Read!"**

*Visit www.icanread.com for information
on enriching your child's reading experience.*

Baby Shark: The Shark Tooth Fairy

Copyright © 2020 by Smart Study Co., Ltd. All rights reserved.

Pinkfong® and Baby Shark™ are licensed trademarks of Smart Study Co., Ltd.

© 2020 Viacom International Inc. All rights reserved.

Nickelodeon is a trademark of Viacom International Inc.

All rights reserved. Printed in the United States of America.

No part of this book may be used or reproduced in any manner whatsoever without written

permission except in the case of brief quotations embodied in critical articles and reviews.

For information address HarperCollins Children's Books, a division of HarperCollins Publishers,

195 Broadway, New York, NY 10007.

www.icanread.com

Library of Congress Control Number: 2020937099

ISBN 978-0-06-304284-1

20 21 22 23 24 LSCC 10 9 8 7 6 5 4 3 2 1

❖

First Edition

My First SHARED READING · I Can Read!

pinkfong
BABY SHARK™

The Shark
Tooth Fairy

HARPER
An Imprint of HarperCollinsPublishers

Baby Shark Family & Friends

**Baby
Shark**

**Mommy
Shark**

**Daddy
Shark**

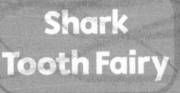

Shark Tooth Fairy

Grandma Shark

Grandpa Shark

5

"Good morning!"
says Baby Shark.
Baby Shark smiles.
Something is
different.

Baby Shark's tooth is gone!
Baby Shark lost his tooth.

10

Baby Shark does not
like to lose things.
He will look
for his lost tooth!

Baby Shark looks
around the sandcastle.
The tooth is not there.

Baby Shark looks
under a rock.
The tooth is not there.

"Has anyone found
my tooth?"
cries Baby Shark.
Baby Shark is afraid
to tell Mommy Shark
that he lost his tooth.

Will Mommy Shark be mad?

Will she be scared?

Or will Mommy Shark

be happy?

Baby Shark doesn't know!

17

That night, Baby Shark
has a bad dream.
He dreams he lost
all his teeth.

He was toothless
like Grandma Shark!

When Baby Shark wakes up,
he is sad.
He needs to tell Mommy.

Baby Shark swims
to Mommy Shark.
"Mommy, my tooth is gone!"
he says.

Mommy Shark hugs
Baby Shark.
She is happy.

"It's okay,"
says Mommy Shark.
"The shark tooth fairy
must have taken it."

23

Mommy Shark smiles.
"Shark tooth fairy takes
your baby teeth.

Then she puts a coin
under your pillow."

That night, Baby Shark

falls asleep.

Then the shark tooth fairy

comes!

The shark tooth fairy
leaves a coin under
Baby Shark's pillow.
Mommy Shark was right!
When Baby Shark wakes up,
he is so happy.

Baby Shark swims
to Mommy Shark.
"Mommy, look!
I've got a shiny coin!"

"Wow!" says Mommy Shark.
"And in time, you will grow
a new tooth."

Thank you,
shark tooth fairy!